OLD HOUSE
NEW HOUSE

A CHILD'S EXPLORATION OF AMERICAN ARCHITECTURAL STYLES

OLD HOUSE

NEW HOUSE

A CHILD'S EXPLORATION OF AMERICAN ARCHITECTURAL STYLES

Written by

MICHAEL GAUGHENBAUGH and HERBERT CAMBURN

Illustrated by

HERBERT CAMBURN

E. F. Sharr
Photographer

THE PRESERVATION PRESS

National Trust for Historic Preservation

The Preservation Press
National Trust for Historic Preservation
1785 Massachusetts Avenue, N.W.
Washington, D.C. 20036

Support is provided by membership dues, contributions, and a matching grant from the National Park Service, U.S. Department of the Interior, under provisions of the National Historic Preservation Act of 1966. The opinions expressed here do not necessarily reflect the views or policies of the Interior Department.

Printed in Hong Kong
97 96 95 94 93   5 4 3 2 1

Library of Congress Cataloging-in-Publication Data

Gaughenbaugh, Michael.
      Old house, new house: a child's exploration of American architectural styles / written by Michael Gaughenbaugh and Herbert Camburn: illustrated by Herbert Camburn.
          p.   cm.
      Summary: As a family restores the large old house they have bought, they learn about its history and special features and about other types of houses, from San Francisco Victorians to Midwest farmhouses to New York brownstones.
      ISBN 0-89133-236-7
      1. Architecture—United States—Themes, motives—Juvenile literature. [1. Architecture, Domestic—History. 2. Dwellings—Conservation and restoration.] I. Camburn, Herbert, ill. II. Title.
NA705.G28 1993   93-1393
728'.0973—dc20   CIP

Designed and composed in Palatino with Bookman
by Dana Levy, Perpetua Press, Los Angeles, California

Preface

AMERICAN HOUSES are wonderful things. They reflect our history, our rich combination of cultural heritages, our changing nation's fashions and ideals, and they illustrate our pride of craftsmanship and technical developments. Whether they are small or large, in any area of America, houses reflect our personalities and attitudes—what we think of ourselves and what we want others to think of us. They are architectural expressions of our social position, hopes, dreams, and goals.

Houses are remarkable places to explore and often reveal delightful surprises both inside and out, including loving, painstaking craftsmanship and ingenious innovations. Our story is one family's adventure in exploring the past. Several historic homes have been used as the basis of the illustrations for this book. The history of the houses and owners, however, has been fictionalized for the purposes of the narrative. We hope that the spirit of these wonderful old homes has been treated with the respect they deserve.

I'M DAVID HOUSTON and my family just bought a new house, but it's old and in very bad shape and it sure isn't very modern. That's Mom and Dad with the real estate agent on the steps. Dad calls the house a "great Midwestern Victorian." Mom calls Dad "crazy!" Dad's a very clever carpenter, and he's going to do what he calls "restore" it. There's really a lot of work to do. Dad says getting the house restored will be an adventure.

When my sister, Lisa, and I went through the house the first time, it felt like we were exploring a castle. This house was so totally different from the one we'd been living in. There were 16 rooms on three floors, plus a basement, and the bedrooms were huge! Some of the rooms had special names we'd never heard of. Mom explained. The pantry was where the china was stored and where the servants (can you imagine us having servants?) could get things ready to serve; a front parlor was an extra living room for special occasions; a conservatory was just for plants. There also was a room for sewing and a nursery for children to live and play in while they were small, and, of course, a library stored all the books. Best of all, way up on the top floor was a ballroom, with a billiard table and lots of space for parties and dancing.

The first time we saw the house it was sort of scary. It smelled damp and musty because it had been empty for a long time. The electricity was off, so there were all sorts of funny, dark spaces and halls. Wallpaper was peeling from the walls, and piles of junk and papers were everywhere. We went up and down two sets of stairs: a fancy staircase in the front hall for the family's use and a narrow, steep one in the back by the kitchen used mainly by the servants.

The eight fireplaces were blocked up, and old, worn linoleum covered almost all of the floors. Some parts of the house seemed newer. Dad said these had been additions, built later than the main house. He showed us where partitions had been used to divide big rooms into smaller ones and where the closed-in front porch had been added by previous owners who had run a restaurant here. The fire escape was added when the house became a nursing home.

So we began our adventure by first buying the house! I know my friends will be excited to visit. They don't live in anything like it. We're not going to move in until a lot of work has been done. Dad says that we'll all have to help. It sounded like a lot of work, but it'll be great when it's all done.

T HE HOUSE IS REALLY OLD—over 100
years. Mom and Dad decided if
they were going to restore the
house and make it like new, they would
take their time and do it right. First, they
needed advice, so Dad hired a restoration
architect, Joshua Peters (he let us call him
Josh). Josh was like an archeologist. He could
figure out how the house originally
looked—even find out the colors it had been
painted 100 years ago.

One of the first things we all did was
carefully check the foundation, walls, and
roof. We discovered a water problem
caused by broken and missing slate shingles
on the roof, which would need to be fixed
right away.

Then, we began our research at the local historical society where we were excited
to discover old photographs of our house
when it was first built in 1870. Records located at the town hall uncovered important
dates related to the house and its changes.
Some former owners as well as neighbors
also gave us ideas of how the house had
changed.

From Josh's research we discovered that

E. F. Sharr
Photographer

the first owners—the family of a local doctor—loved and improved the house until 1905. Then the records showed that the last of the family moved away in 1928. It was converted into a funeral home in 1930. Thirty years later, in 1960, it became a nursing home and was changed in a major way: a two-story addition was put on with smaller bedrooms as well as the fire escape. Finally in 1975 it was sold to people who

House Photo Dates

✓ New in 1870
✓ Last Family Photo
   From 1905
✓ Funeral Home.
   1930
✓ Convalescent
   Home 1960
✓ Restaurant 1975

turned it into a restaurant. They enlarged the kitchen and enclosed the porch to make more dining space.

Dad, Mom, and Josh wanted to restore the house to its original look so it could show its graceful old age. This would mean removing all of the "misguided additions and modernizations," according to Josh.

9

AFTER THE ROOF WAS REPAIRED, we began work on the inside, first by hauling out the junk that had been left behind. We all helped, but Lisa and I weren't allowed to be around areas where workers were removing asbestos and layers of old, lead-based paint, which Dad said was very toxic.

That's me picking up the old linoleum. Underneath I discovered wonderful oak parquet floors with borders inlaid with geometric patterns of dark walnut. Oak floors that were exposed we covered with dropcloths for protection until the dirty work was done.

Water coming in through the leaking roof had caused some damage to the plaster on several interior walls. Plaster is being patched in this room; where plaster has broken away you can see the lath, or wood strips, that support the plaster.

Josh took paint samples to test for lead and study the colors. He said we were lucky; most of the oak woodwork on the hall and parlor walls had only been varnished. Still, in some rooms, there were 10 coats of paint to remove and eight layers of wallpaper to steam off. Boy, was some of it ugly! When it came off, so did part of the cracked plaster. Dust was everywhere. Mom said it would take months to clean up.

Dad showed us special oak

pocket doors that slid into the walls between rooms—
they just disappeared. You can see one here on the
right. When closed, the doors kept a room quiet and
protected from drafts. We were lucky the doors had sur-
vived all of the alterations and still had their brass door
pulls.

Dad and the workers took down all the modern
light fixtures. Old gas chandeliers that Dad had found
stored away in the attic would be put back in place.
Dad said that we would electrify them first.

My special discovery was old bottles
and a note hidden in the wall near the staircase behind some broken
plaster. The note said, "I
helped build this house. I
hope you like my work.
Eben Clark, 1870." I felt
like Eben Clark had writ-
ten that note especially
for me!

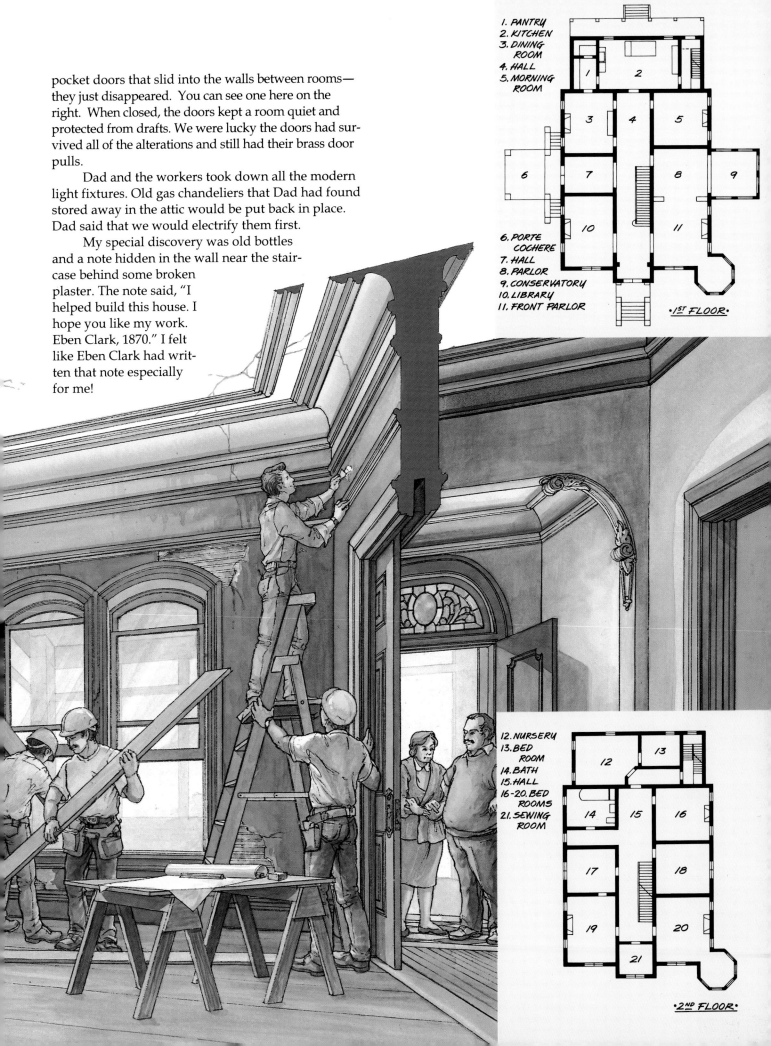

1. PANTRY
2. KITCHEN
3. DINING ROOM
4. HALL
5. MORNING ROOM
6. PORTE COCHERE
7. HALL
8. PARLOR
9. CONSERVATORY
10. LIBRARY
11. FRONT PARLOR

·1ST FLOOR·

12. NURSERY
13. BED ROOM
14. BATH
15. HALL
16-20. BED ROOMS
21. SEWING ROOM

·2ND FLOOR·

I WAS REALLY EXCITED when the work on the outside of the house began. Mr. Rivera, the contractor, and Josh had carefully worked out a plan. The newer additions had to be torn down before they could really start to preserve and restore the older parts of the house.

Josh told us the proper name for the house's style was Second Empire, referring to buildings built in France in the 1800s. The roof shape was called a mansard after an architect for the French king, Louis XIV, way back when America was still a bunch of colonies. Josh thought the house was "architecturally significant," which meant it was an important example of its style and detail. He suggested that Dad apply to have the house included in the National Register of Historic Places, a special list kept by the National Park Service in Washington, D.C. Just imagine! We might be living in a "registered historic house!"

The workers put up scaffolding and began to carefully tear down the additions, such as the porch and fire escape. On the roof, broken and missing slate shingles had been replaced with slate. While it had been expensive to use slate, according to Dad, in the long run using this brittle but weather-resistant stone would make a good strong roof that would last a long time and one that looked right on the house.

Along the top edges of the roof, the remains of the cresting (decorative ironwork in a lacy pattern) were removed as well. Mr. Rivera also had to take away window sash and decorative brackets under the eaves, along with other trim, for restoration. Any pieces that were missing would be carefully reproduced to match the old ones. All of the old trim would be put back in place later when the house was put back together. There were so many pieces, they looked like a giant jigsaw puzzle, but Josh kept track of them all on the drawings he had made of the house.

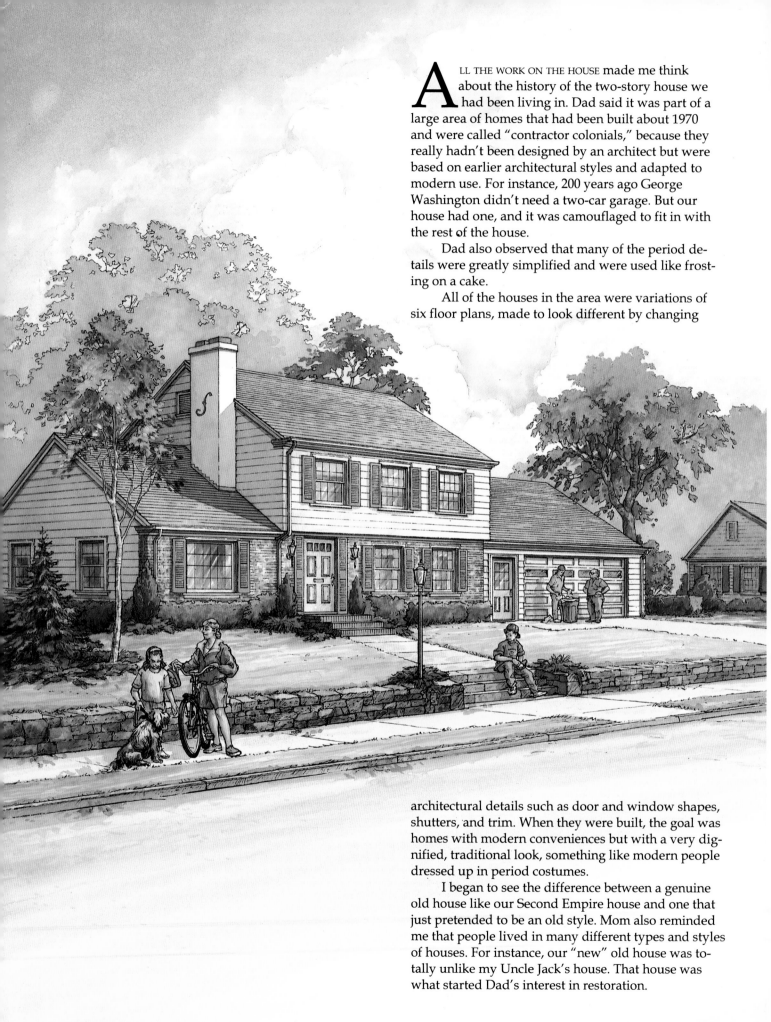

ALL THE WORK ON THE HOUSE made me think about the history of the two-story house we had been living in. Dad said it was part of a large area of homes that had been built about 1970 and were called "contractor colonials," because they really hadn't been designed by an architect but were based on earlier architectural styles and adapted to modern use. For instance, 200 years ago George Washington didn't need a two-car garage. But our house had one, and it was camouflaged to fit in with the rest of the house.

Dad also observed that many of the period details were greatly simplified and were used like frosting on a cake.

All of the houses in the area were variations of six floor plans, made to look different by changing

architectural details such as door and window shapes, shutters, and trim. When they were built, the goal was homes with modern conveniences but with a very dignified, traditional look, something like modern people dressed up in period costumes.

I began to see the difference between a genuine old house like our Second Empire house and one that just pretended to be an old style. Mom also reminded me that people lived in many different types and styles of houses. For instance, our "new" old house was totally unlike my Uncle Jack's house. That house was what started Dad's interest in restoration.

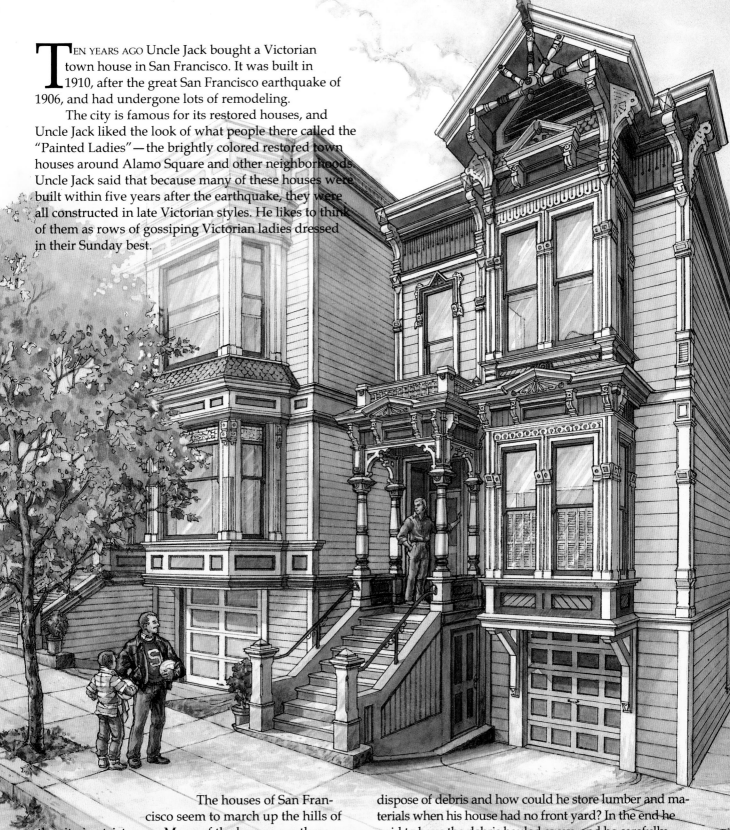

TEN YEARS AGO Uncle Jack bought a Victorian town house in San Francisco. It was built in 1910, after the great San Francisco earthquake of 1906, and had undergone lots of remodeling.

The city is famous for its restored houses, and Uncle Jack liked the look of what people there called the "Painted Ladies"—the brightly colored restored town houses around Alamo Square and other neighborhoods. Uncle Jack said that because many of these houses were built within five years after the earthquake, they were all constructed in late Victorian styles. He likes to think of them as rows of gossiping Victorian ladies dressed in their Sunday best.

The houses of San Francisco seem to march up the hills of the city in strict rows. Many of the houses are three stories tall—long and thin, like tall railroad cars. They are all very close together but not attached. The front of the lots are very narrow and small, and garages, if there are any, are located under the houses. Most of the houses have big bay windows overlooking the streets.

Uncle Jack's house took five years to restore, and he had all sorts of problems. Where in the city could he

dispose of debris and how could he store lumber and materials when his house had no front yard? In the end he paid to have the debris hauled away, and he carefully planned to have materials delivered only when he knew he was going to use them.

Inside, Uncle Jack has restored all of the Victorian details and moldings. He even found wallpaper and drapery fabrics that were reproductions of styles from 1910. I especially liked the old bathrooms with their tiny tiles and the iron bathtubs with funny ball-and-claw feet. Dad thought if Uncle Jack could do it, he could too!

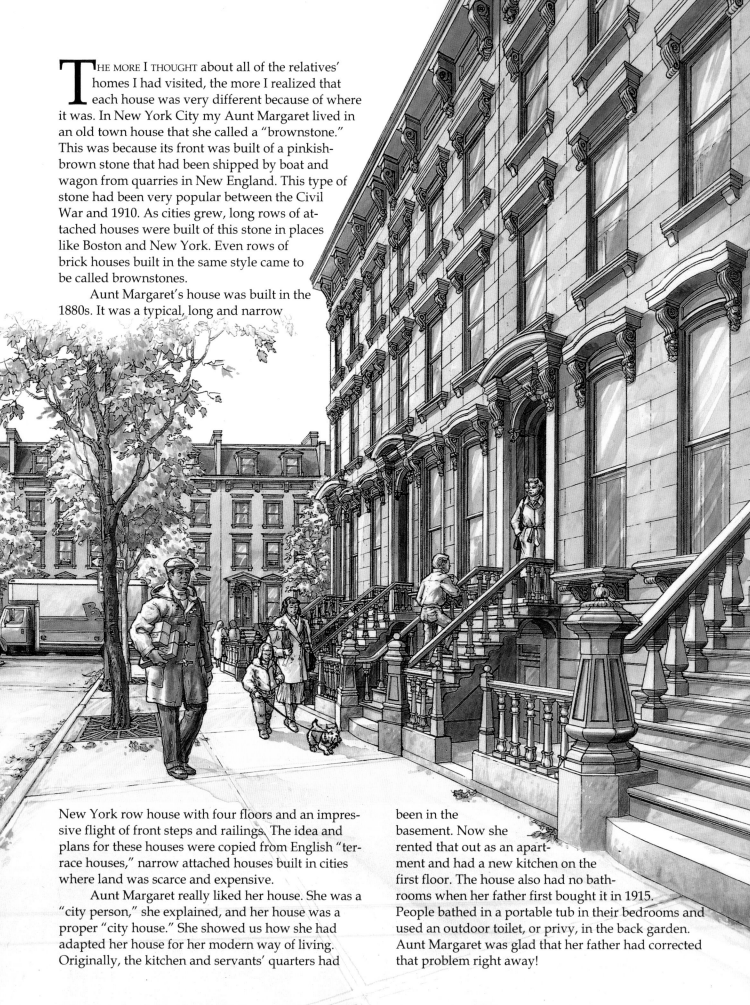

THE MORE I THOUGHT about all of the relatives' homes I had visited, the more I realized that each house was very different because of where it was. In New York City my Aunt Margaret lived in an old town house that she called a "brownstone." This was because its front was built of a pinkish-brown stone that had been shipped by boat and wagon from quarries in New England. This type of stone had been very popular between the Civil War and 1910. As cities grew, long rows of attached houses were built of this stone in places like Boston and New York. Even rows of brick houses built in the same style came to be called brownstones.

Aunt Margaret's house was built in the 1880s. It was a typical, long and narrow New York row house with four floors and an impressive flight of front steps and railings. The idea and plans for these houses were copied from English "terrace houses," narrow attached houses built in cities where land was scarce and expensive.

Aunt Margaret really liked her house. She was a "city person," she explained, and her house was a proper "city house." She showed us how she had adapted her house for her modern way of living. Originally, the kitchen and servants' quarters had been in the basement. Now she rented that out as an apartment and had a new kitchen on the first floor. The house also had no bathrooms when her father first bought it in 1915. People bathed in a portable tub in their bedrooms and used an outdoor toilet, or privy, in the back garden. Aunt Margaret was glad that her father had corrected that problem right away!

MY COUSINS' HOUSE was totally different because they lived on a farm. In the country there was lots of space for a house, garden, and yard. Their home was built in 1915, after the first farmhouse had burned. The new house was in the Dutch Colonial Revival style, which copied the houses built by early Dutch settlers on the East Coast. It had a special roof shape called a gambrel. Dad explained that this allowed for lots of space under the roof. Even barns often used this roof shape to make room for big hay lofts.

This style of house was also built in towns, but there it would have been very close to the neighboring houses. My cousins' closest neighbor lived a half-mile away. Hardly any crowding here!

Lisa and I always enjoyed visiting the farm. We loved roaming around watching all the animals and exploring the different farm buildings. It was so different

from the city—lots of open space and interesting smells, no street noise or smog, and huge trees everywhere.

On the farm the house is the hub of a business— home, office, and work all in one. You didn't have to commute—your work was just outside your back door, and you could have lunch at home. My cousins always had important chores to help with around the farm.

They traveled to school by bus. In winter they were sometimes snowed in. I always thought being snowbound would be a great adventure. But the city still has advantages. Shopping is a lot handier, and friends are closer. In fact, I guess we really have it pretty easy in the city, considering all the work my cousins had to do on the farm all year.

THE HOUSE WHERE DAD GREW UP looked pretty modern to me compared with my cousins' farmhouse. That's it below with Grandma on the porch. Granddad called his house a ranch house, and he built it in 1948. Right after World War II soldiers returning home and starting families had trouble finding places to live. Houses were expensive and apartments were scarce. People had to think about ways to build houses quickly and cheaply. Veterans' benefits, like GI loans, helped many returning soldiers to build or buy homes. There was an explosion of house building all across the country. Homes seemed to spring up overnight to meet the needs of young married couples.

Granddad said the first of these new inexpensive homes was located in tract developments like Levittown on Long Island, New York, and Lakewood

in Southern California. In Levittown, 6,000 new houses were spread over 2,400 acres, and in Lakewood, 13,000 homes were built at the rate of 150 a week! Most cities had developments like these, where houses costing between $4,000 and $8,000 were considered a bargain.

Grandma remembered that to appeal to young couples, developers built houses that had ultra-modern interiors and exteriors that were variations of early American or "modern" styles—adapted Cape Cod cottages in the East and California ranch houses all over the country but especially in the Midwest and West. Most ranch houses like Granddad's were one story and built very close together. They had standardized floor plans that

18

made these houses easy and economical to build.

Young couples of the 1950s loved the ranch house. Everyone liked the open space, sunshine, patios, and barbecues. Ranch houses had gently sloping roofs and oversize picture windows. They were either long or U-shaped, with patios in back. I liked another new idea in Granddad's house—a split-level interior, where different rooms were a few steps above or below other rooms. One of these special spaces was the game room, rec room, or rumpus room, a more noisy area often located on the lower level. Now we'd call this the family room, but when Granddad built his split-level, it was a new idea.

Grandma said when she moved in, Dad was a baby and she had her hands full. Like all of her friends, she depended on ideas from pictures in popular magazines like the *Ladies' Home Journal* and *Good Housekeeping*.

SPLIT LEVEL HOUSE - 1959

With houses so much alike, it was difficult to make the inside and outside of your home look different from your neighbor's.

Dad said it was great growing up in the 1950s. His family had one of the first television sets in his neighborhood and he watched the *Lone Ranger* cowboy show every week (he even dressed up as the Lone Ranger one Halloween). He loved rock-and-roll, although my Grandma disapproved, and he was especially fascinated with stories about flying saucers. (Dad remembers the important things!) Granddad and Grandma still live in their ranch house, and we still cook on the barbecue that Dad helped to build.

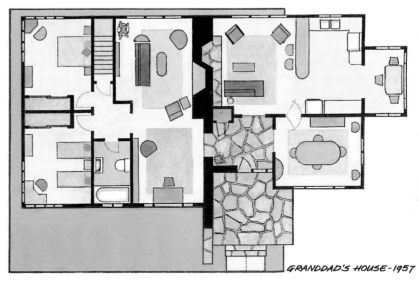

GRANDDAD'S HOUSE - 1957

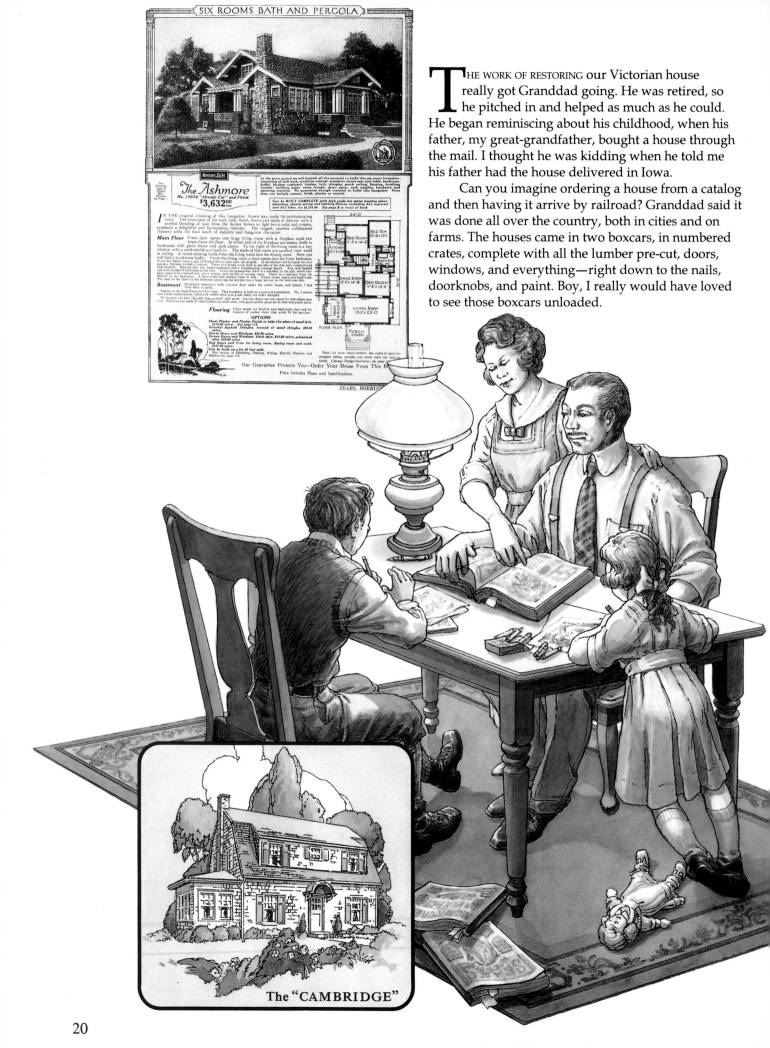

THE WORK OF RESTORING our Victorian house really got Granddad going. He was retired, so he pitched in and helped as much as he could. He began reminiscing about his childhood, when his father, my great-grandfather, bought a house through the mail. I thought he was kidding when he told me his father had the house delivered in Iowa.

Can you imagine ordering a house from a catalog and then having it arrive by railroad? Granddad said it was done all over the country, both in cities and on farms. The houses came in two boxcars, in numbered crates, complete with all the lumber pre-cut, doors, windows, and everything—right down to the nails, doorknobs, and paint. Boy, I really would have loved to see those boxcars unloaded.

Granddad told us his house story. After they were married in 1912, my great-grandfather and great-grandmother worked very hard to save enough money to buy a house. He worked 11-hour days, six days a week, for $2.20 a day. That only came to about $700 a year! It was difficult to save much on those wages, and after my grandfather and his sister were born, it was even harder. It took 12 years before the family could afford a building lot and save $300 for the downpayment on a house. Even then, the monthly house payments would be around $25.

By 1924 several companies were selling mail-order houses. My great-grandfather ordered all the catalogs. Long evenings were spent sitting at the dining room table after supper studying the different house models, while Granddad did his lessons and his sister colored the catalogs. Deciding what the family could

The "KENWOOD"

making decisions was difficult. Granddad said his family's choice had been the "Ashmore," a bungalow-style house. My great-grandfather still worried about the cost, because the price didn't include plastering and cement work. After several letters, Sears agreed to simplify the floor plan, which actually gave the family more floor space and cost less. So Granddad's family took the big step and ordered the house.

After placing the order, work began on digging the basement and pouring the foundation. Three months later the first boxcar of materials arrived from the lumber mill. Granddad said it was exciting to see the house grow. With hard work and the help of friends, the mail-order home was finished in six months. It still looks just like the picture in the Sears catalog.

The "DEVONSHIRE"

afford was a major decision and took over nine months.

Granddad showed me the Sears, Roebuck and Company catalog his father had ordered from (he had saved it all these years!). There were many models and styles to choose from at prices ranging from $800 to $3,000. There were modest homes in pretty, picturesque styles, such as bungalows with wide overhanging eaves, and modern colonials in one-story cottages and big, two-story versions. Different models had wonderful romantic names such as the "Del Rey" and the "Ivanhoe," while others had dignified names such as the "Concord" or the "Richmond."

Many of the models offered choices of floor plans and options such as "Oak Doors and Trim for $148.00 Extra." There were almost too many choices—

The "MAYFLOWER"

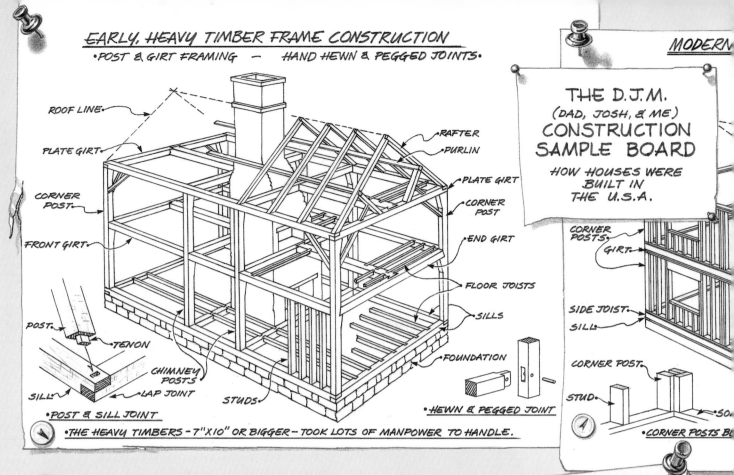

EARLY, HEAVY TIMBER FRAME CONSTRUCTION
•POST & GIRT FRAMING — HAND HEWN & PEGGED JOINTS•

ROOF LINE•

PLATE GIRT•

CORNER POST•

FRONT GIRT•

POST•

TENON

CHIMNEY POSTS•

SILL•

LAP JOINT

STUDS•

•POST & SILL JOINT

•RAFTER
•PURLIN
•PLATE GIRT
•CORNER POST
•END GIRT
•FLOOR JOISTS
•SILLS
•FOUNDATION

•HEWN & PEGGED JOINT

•THE HEAVY TIMBERS – 7"X10" OR BIGGER – TOOK LOTS OF MANPOWER TO HANDLE.

THE D.J.M.
(DAD, JOSH, & ME)
CONSTRUCTION SAMPLE BOARD
HOW HOUSES WERE BUILT IN THE U.S.A.

CORNER POSTS•
GIRT•
SIDE JOIST•
SILL•
CORNER POST•
STUD•
SO

•CORNER POSTS B

I DIDN'T REALLY UNDERSTAND how 150 houses could be built in one week in tracts like Levittown after World War II. So Josh helped me and Dad create a special board to show the many ways that houses have been constructed in America. We copied pages from books about construction we found in the library and Josh shared some of his books with us.

Josh explained that people have used lots of different methods and materials over time, but they depended on what was inexpensive and easily available. That's why log cabins were built on the frontier where huge forests grew, while sod houses dominated the prairies where trees were scarce. In areas where supplies of wood and clay existed, bricks were made. The wood fueled the brick kilns or ovens that baked the clay bricks. Because there is so little wood in the Southwest, sun-dried adobe bricks were the chief building material. In many states, plain stone found on the ground, called fieldstone, made good sturdy walls, foundations, and chimneys.

Josh pointed out that in the United States, where most houses are wood, the speed a house could be built depended on how the structural frame, or skeleton, was put up. I'd never thought of a house as having "bones" before, but Dad said that the frame of a house was really like a skeleton. The outer "skin" could be made of all sorts of materials—brick or stone, wood siding, stucco, or shingles.

Our special board showed how early houses were built of heavy, hand-hewn timbers. Nails were handmade and expensive, so joints were fitted and secured with wood pegs—a very slow and precise process. And

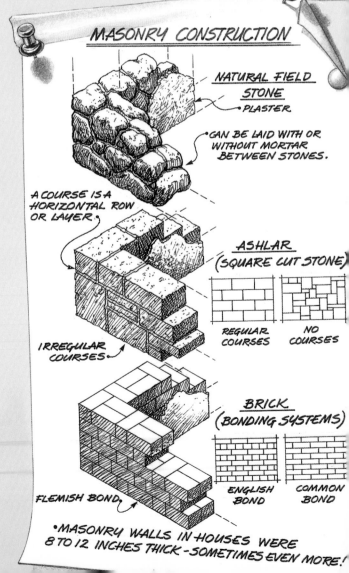

MASONRY CONSTRUCTION

NATURAL FIELD STONE
•PLASTER
•CAN BE LAID WITH OR WITHOUT MORTAR BETWEEN STONES.

A COURSE IS A HORIZONTAL ROW OR LAYER•

IRREGULAR COURSES•

ASHLAR (SQUARE CUT STONE)
REGULAR COURSES   NO COURSES

BRICK (BONDING SYSTEMS)
ENGLISH BOND   COMMON BOND
FLEMISH BOND•

•MASONRY WALLS IN HOUSES WERE 8 TO 12 INCHES THICK – SOMETIMES EVEN MORE!

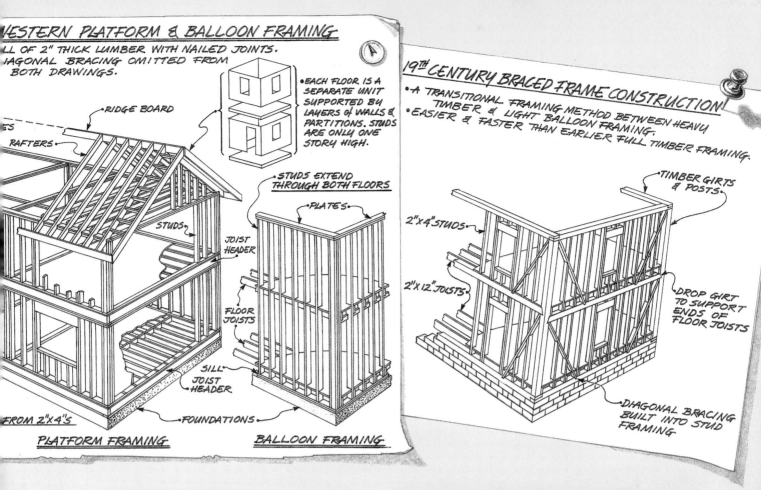

WESTERN PLATFORM & BALLOON FRAMING

ALL OF 2" THICK LUMBER WITH NAILED JOINTS.
DIAGONAL BRACING OMITTED FROM BOTH DRAWINGS.

• EACH FLOOR IS A SEPARATE UNIT SUPPORTED BY LAYERS OF WALLS & PARTITIONS. STUDS ARE ONLY ONE STORY HIGH.

- RIDGE BOARD
- RAFTERS
- STUDS
- JOIST HEADER
- FLOOR JOISTS
- SILL JOIST HEADER
- FROM 2"X4"S
- FOUNDATIONS

PLATFORM FRAMING

• STUDS EXTEND THROUGH BOTH FLOORS
- PLATES

BALLOON FRAMING

19TH CENTURY BRACED FRAME CONSTRUCTION!

• A TRANSITIONAL FRAMING METHOD BETWEEN HEAVY TIMBER & LIGHT BALLOON FRAMING.
• EASIER & FASTER THAN EARLIER FULL TIMBER FRAMING.

- TIMBER GIRTS & POSTS
- 2"X4" STUDS
- 2"X12" JOISTS
- DROP GIRT TO SUPPORT ENDS OF FLOOR JOISTS
- DIAGONAL BRACING BUILT INTO STUD FRAMING

the heavy timbers required lots of men to raise them in place. As water- and steam-powered sawmills grew in number, machine-sawn lumber became more available about 1800, making it possible for builders to construct houses more simply by combining timbers with standard two-by-four-inch lumber. Josh called this "braced-frame construction."

In the 1830s a new fast, lightweight method of building was developed with the aid of machine-made nails.

This system was called "balloon framing," because it consisted of a strong, lightweight shell, made completely of machine-sawn, two-inch-thick lumber. Joints didn't have to be hand hewn, and fewer men could lift the wall frames.

I could see how it was easy to build these new houses in Levittown. The floor plans were all similar, and the one-story houses could be built by an assembly-line process. Our sample board helped it all make sense.

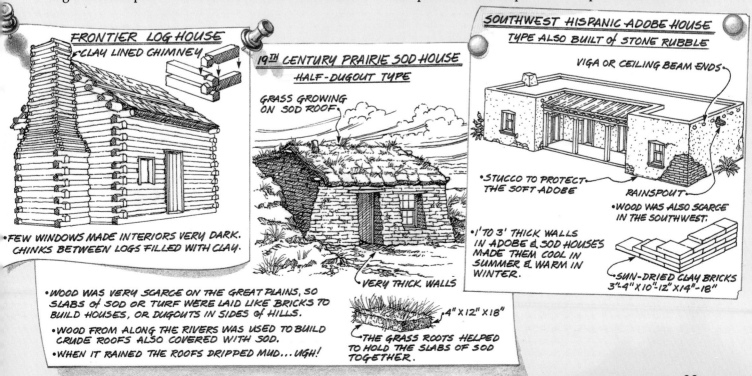

FRONTIER LOG HOUSE

• CLAY LINED CHIMNEY

• FEW WINDOWS MADE INTERIORS VERY DARK. CHINKS BETWEEN LOGS FILLED WITH CLAY.

• WOOD WAS VERY SCARCE ON THE GREAT PLAINS, SO SLABS OF SOD OR TURF WERE LAID LIKE BRICKS TO BUILD HOUSES, OR DUGOUTS IN SIDES OF HILLS.
• WOOD FROM ALONG THE RIVERS WAS USED TO BUILD CRUDE ROOFS ALSO COVERED WITH SOD.
• WHEN IT RAINED THE ROOFS DRIPPED MUD...UGH!

19TH CENTURY PRAIRIE SOD HOUSE
HALF-DUGOUT TYPE

- GRASS GROWING ON SOD ROOF
- VERY THICK WALLS
- 4"X 12"X 18"
- THE GRASS ROOTS HELPED TO HOLD THE SLABS OF SOD TOGETHER.

SOUTHWEST HISPANIC ADOBE HOUSE
TYPE ALSO BUILT OF STONE RUBBLE

- VIGA OR CEILING BEAM ENDS
- STUCCO TO PROTECT THE SOFT ADOBE
- RAINSPOUT
- 1' TO 3' THICK WALLS IN ADOBE & SOD HOUSES MADE THEM COOL IN SUMMER & WARM IN WINTER.
- WOOD WAS ALSO SCARCE IN THE SOUTHWEST.
- SUN-DRIED CLAY BRICKS 3"-4"X10"-12"X14"-18"

GRANDDAD RECALLED what the inside of his parent's house was like after it was finished in 1925. His mother had secretly saved pennies from her grocery money to have a "little extra" to help decorate the new mail-order house. In 12 years she had saved nearly $90 for wallpaper and fabric for curtains and slipcovers. This was a secret between her and Granddad. While they would have to make do with most of the hand-me-down furniture that had come from both sides of their families, my

floor. The old oak icebox (they lasted forever) was put out on the screened-in porch. My great-grandmother was happiest with her new, green porcelain-enameled gas range—you didn't even have to bend over to take things out of the oven. And her fondest wish was answered: as a special surprise, my great-grandfather had secretly installed a gas water heater in the basement to supply hot running water.

With its yellow curtains, the new kitchen was bright and sunny. The old kitchen furniture was

great-grandparents planned to buy a new gas range and, maybe, a davenport suite for the living room. My great-grandmother's most private wish—and one she felt the family couldn't afford—was for hot running water in the house.

The new kitchen was a modern wonder. There were built-in cabinets, counter space on each side of the sink, and a built-in cottage breakfast nook, just like the ones shown in the *Ladies' Home Journal*. Granddad said he loved the nook—it was a comfortable place for him to study while his mother baked on Saturdays.

There were other special features, such as an ironing board that folded down out of the wall and genuine inlaid linoleum on both the counters and the

painted in bright enamel to make it look new. I think Granddad likes kitchens, just like I do. They're very friendly places.

The living room had a real fireplace and was filled with light from its big windows. My great-grandmother's hand-sewn cretonne slipcovers made the old armchairs and wicker rocker look cheerful against the new Wilton carpet that had been a house-warming gift. My great-grandparents kept the old piano and phonograph in the living room and owned the only crystal radio set on the block.

This house also had an inside bathroom; many people didn't, especially on farms. The walls were tiled, and there was even a shower with a curtain. Granddad said he loved his first shower. He had always

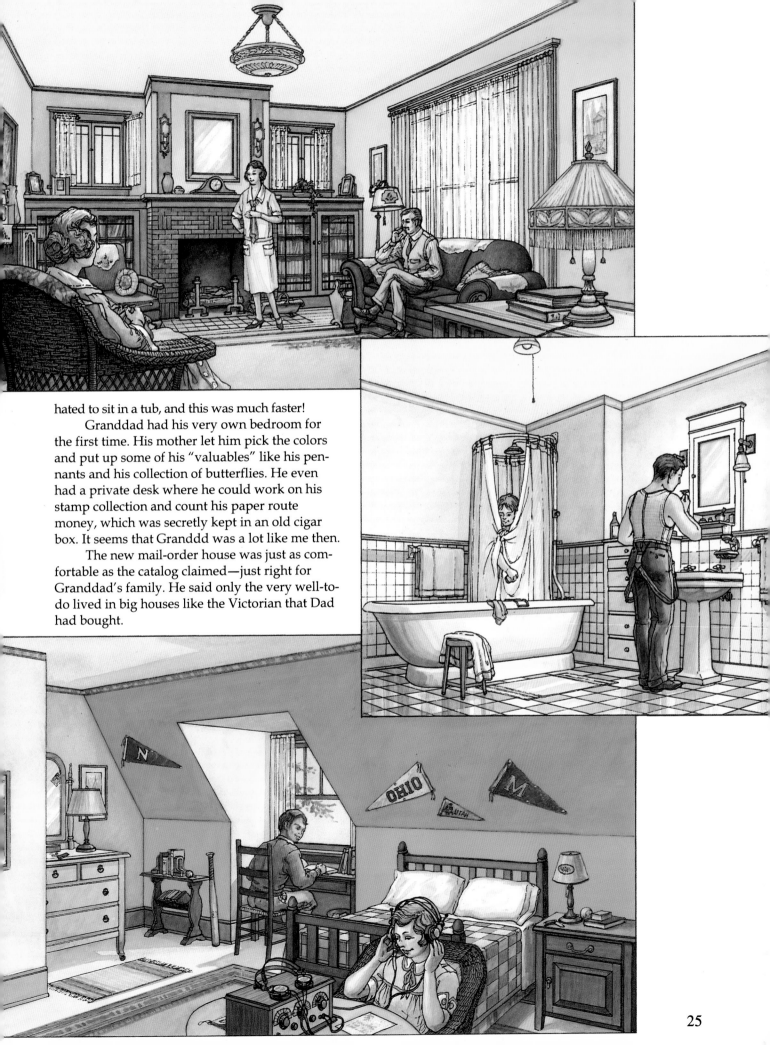

hated to sit in a tub, and this was much faster!

Granddad had his very own bedroom for the first time. His mother let him pick the colors and put up some of his "valuables" like his pennants and his collection of butterflies. He even had a private desk where he could work on his stamp collection and count his paper route money, which was secretly kept in an old cigar box. It seems that Granddd was a lot like me then.

The new mail-order house was just as comfortable as the catalog claimed—just right for Granddad's family. He said only the very well-to-do lived in big houses like the Victorian that Dad had bought.

DAD SAID THE INSIDE of our big Victorian house in 1890 would have seemed very different from Granddad's house in 1925. Ours had lots of living space—16 rooms with high, 12-foot ceilings, plus hallways and bathrooms. There were even servants' quarters in the house and outside over the carriage house.

Because the house had no electricity when it was built, it would have been lighted by oil or gas lamps. These would have been very dangerous to handle, especially for children. Fires were a very real problem.

We made another discovery—the original, rusty

from their own well in case something went wrong. Irons had to be heated on the stove for ironing all year round. There wasn't much counter or cupboard space, but the pantry off the kitchen had storage for the good china and glassware and space for the icebox. In summer an iceman delivered 100 pounds of ice for the icebox, three times a week. Mom said she could really use the pantry now—it was still a good old idea.

Mom explained that the old kitchen, with its metal, zinc-lined sink and oilcloth-covered work table, was the working center of the house, where the

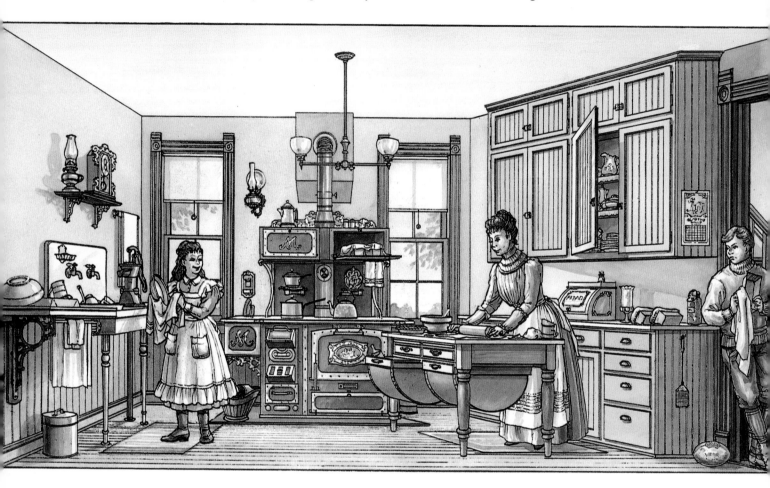

kitchen range stored in the garage attic. Mom said coal stoves made cooking very hard work. The stove had to be kept going all day to fix meals and made the kitchen very hot and uncomfortable, especially in summer. Coal had to be lugged, ashes emptied, and the stove kept polished with "blackening" to keep it from rusting. An old instruction manual we found in the oven bragged:

> *The Majestic Range, the Acme of Scientific and Mechanical Perfection Combined with Common Sense . . . guaranteed to heat 12 gallons of water while breakfast is cooking.*

I guess the family that lived here was lucky to have running water, but there was a backup hand pump

housewife organized her week: Monday was wash day; Tuesday, ironing; Wednesday, sewing and mending; Thursday, dusting and airing; Friday, sweeping and shopping; Saturday, baking and getting Sunday's clothes ready. Sunday was a quiet day for the family, for church or socializing. Housekeeping was a hard, full-time job.

Our huge old bathrooms originally were tiled and had cast-iron tubs on legs or wood-framed copper tubs. The toilets had overhead gravity water closets. Showers rarely existed!

The front parlor was the most formal room and was used only on Sundays and special occasions. The back parlor was a sitting room for everyday use. A piano was very important for entertainment—almost all

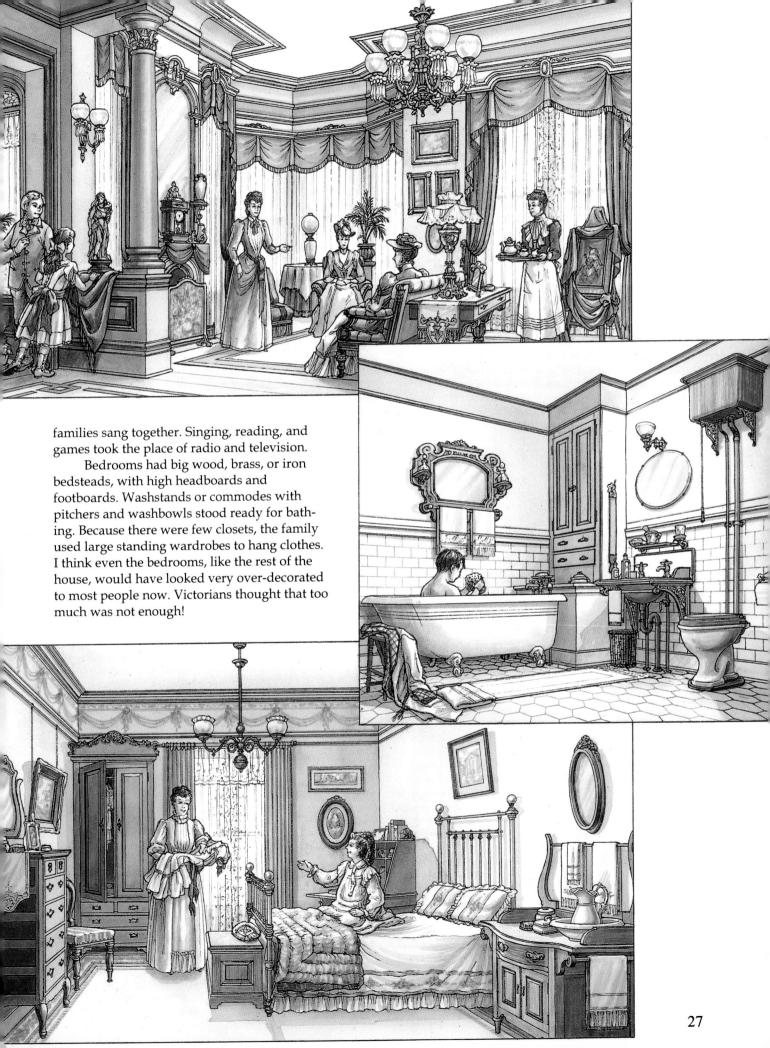

families sang together. Singing, reading, and games took the place of radio and television.

Bedrooms had big wood, brass, or iron bedsteads, with high headboards and footboards. Washstands or commodes with pitchers and washbowls stood ready for bathing. Because there were few closets, the family used large standing wardrobes to hang clothes. I think even the bedrooms, like the rest of the house, would have looked very over-decorated to most people now. Victorians thought that too much was not enough!

When we went on vacation in the Midwest, I saw that the streets of small towns were lined with other kinds of Victorian houses, which Dad called Queen Annes. Josh explained that the Queen Anne style probably was the most varied and popular of the styles of the late Victorian builders. Old pattern books showed that Queen Anne designs used very inventive mixtures of shapes with lots of gables, towers, dormers, and porches. These were made more elaborate by combining different materials—brick, stone, wood, and stucco. The Queen Anne houses were further decorated with lots of ornaments and patterns, from delicate scrollwork to all types of shaped shingles—everything the builder could invent and combine. Josh said the complicated shapes were intended to catch the light and cast shadows in different ways at various times of day. The Queen Anne style really was a spirited, extravagant display of an owner's taste and personality. And these houses were a lot of fun to look at, especially when they were painted a rich range of colors as well.

Mom explained that wide porches, or verandas, were important in everyday life. During hot summers, before air conditioning, these big houses could be very uncomfortable. The porches served as open, shaded rooms where you could sit to catch the breeze and "watch the world pass by" on a long summer's evening or Sunday afternoon. You would have seen every family on the block grouped on these verandas in wicker furniture or porch swings.

The porches were cool places for all kinds of activities: kids obviously played there and meals were eaten there. You could chat with passersby or just listen to the gramophone through the open windows. I can just see families entertaining visitors and serving them lemonade, cooled with chunks of ice chipped from the blocks in the pantry icebox.

At night, when the upstairs bedrooms were very hot, sometimes the children were allowed to sleep outside on the porches, Mom said. I think this would be great fun—you could have long conversations and tell stories in the dark. Of course, there were flies and mosquitoes, but they were just part of summer life, just like the fireflies that were as much a thrill then as they are now.

Granddad said streets often were unpaved—even when he was a boy. Horses and buggies created clouds of dust that came through the screened windows and made housecleaning difficult. He said spray from water-wagons was sometimes used to "lay-the-dust" for holidays and funerals, but the streets soon dried out, and the dust rose again. The dust wouldn't bother me if I had a chance to live in a big Queen Anne house for a summer in 1880.

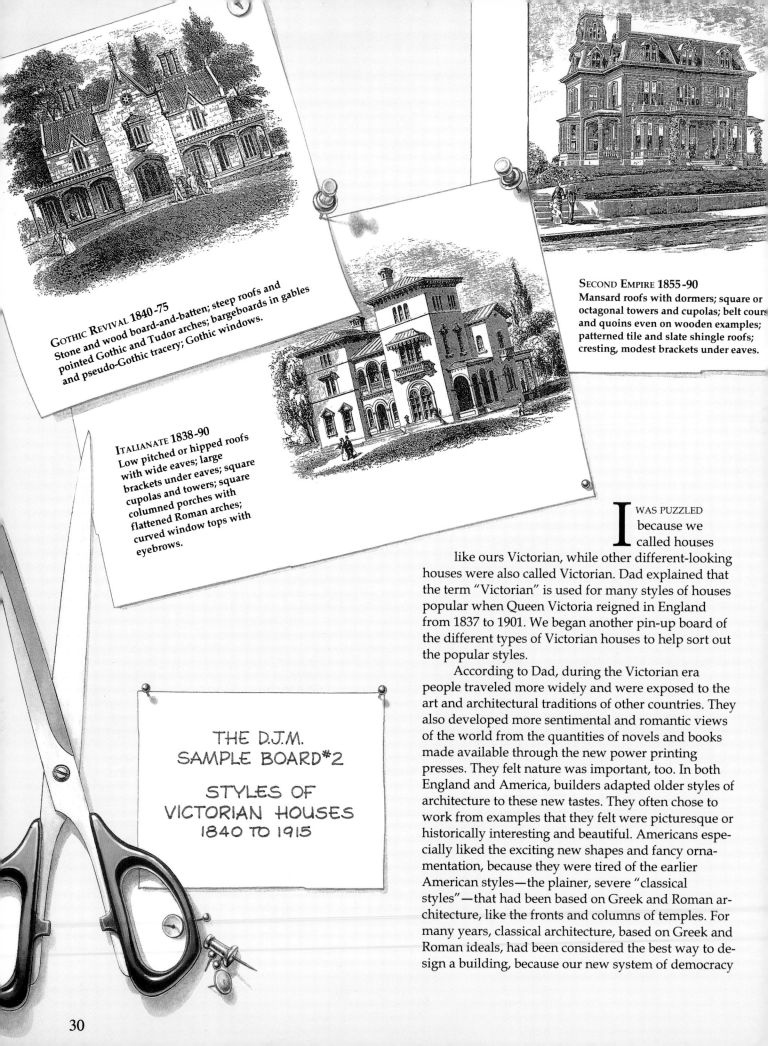

GOTHIC REVIVAL 1840-75
Stone and wood board-and-batten; steep roofs and pointed Gothic and Tudor arches; bargeboards in gables and pseudo-Gothic tracery; Gothic windows.

SECOND EMPIRE 1855-90
Mansard roofs with dormers; square or octagonal towers and cupolas; belt cours and quoins even on wooden examples; patterned tile and slate shingle roofs; cresting, modest brackets under eaves.

ITALIANATE 1838-90
Low pitched or hipped roofs with wide eaves; large brackets under eaves; square cupolas and towers; square columned porches with flattened Roman arches; curved window tops with eyebrows.

THE D.J.M.
SAMPLE BOARD #2

STYLES OF
VICTORIAN HOUSES
1840 TO 1915

I WAS PUZZLED because we called houses like ours Victorian, while other different-looking houses were also called Victorian. Dad explained that the term "Victorian" is used for many styles of houses popular when Queen Victoria reigned in England from 1837 to 1901. We began another pin-up board of the different types of Victorian houses to help sort out the popular styles.

According to Dad, during the Victorian era people traveled more widely and were exposed to the art and architectural traditions of other countries. They also developed more sentimental and romantic views of the world from the quantities of novels and books made available through the new power printing presses. They felt nature was important, too. In both England and America, builders adapted older styles of architecture to these new tastes. They often chose to work from examples that they felt were picturesque or historically interesting and beautiful. Americans especially liked the exciting new shapes and fancy ornamentation, because they were tired of the earlier American styles—the plainer, severe "classical styles"—that had been based on Greek and Roman architecture, like the fronts and columns of temples. For many years, classical architecture, based on Greek and Roman ideals, had been considered the best way to design a building, because our new system of democracy

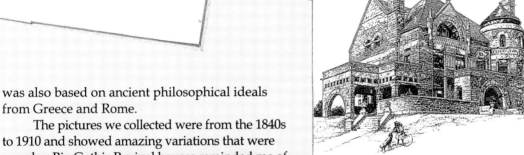

EASTLAKE/STICK STYLE 1855-1910
Steep gabled roofs with Tudor chimneys; complex combinations of rectangular shapes and gables; half-timber effects with vertical, horizontal and diagonal boards; sticklike brackets and turned porch posts.

QUEEN ANNE 1875-1915
Irregular and complex house shapes with round or square towers and turrets; elaborate porches with scrollwork and sawed and turned gingerbread ornament; turned porch posts; decorated gables and porch headers; complex shingle patterns and brackets.

RICHARDSONIAN ROMANESQUE 1870-1905
Inspired by architect Henry Hobson Richardson; massive rustic ashlar stonework with heavy round arches and arcades; round or square towers; stone and brick combinations; slate or tile roofs; heavy squat look.

was also based on ancient philosophical ideals from Greece and Rome.

The pictures we collected were from the 1840s to 1910 and showed amazing variations that were popular. Big Gothic Revival houses reminded me of castles and knights. Italianate homes looked like Italian buildings I had seen in the *National Geographic* magazine. Romanesque houses made me think of fortresses, while Eastlake and Queen Anne buildings seemed to have come from storybooks.

Many of these confusing choices were illustrated in books published by writers like Andrew Jackson Downing, whom Dad called a "building reformer." Downing emphatically wrote in the 1840s that rustic-looking cottages and Italianate villas in earthy colors were more appropriate as homes than stark, white houses with classical columns and details because they did not pretend to be anything else. "A house should look like a house, not a Greek temple," Downing said.

We collected pictures from mail-order pattern books with plans that Dad said were copied by carpenters and masons all across the country. In the 1800s, new power jigsaws and lathes made it easy for carpenters to create decorative "gingerbread" trim for any style of house. You could even update your out-of-fashion house by just adding new trim and details.

SHINGLE STYLE 1880-1905
Shingles covering all wall surfaces; often rough stone foundations; low, rambling forms with varied roof lines; fat, round towers; large porches and minimal decoration.

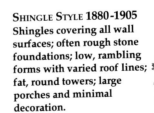

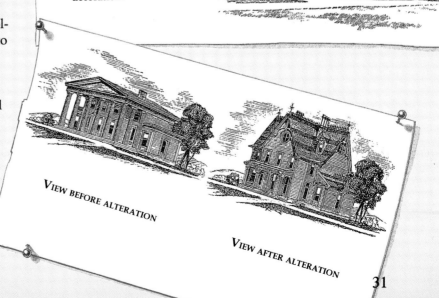

VIEW BEFORE ALTERATION

VIEW AFTER ALTERATION

31

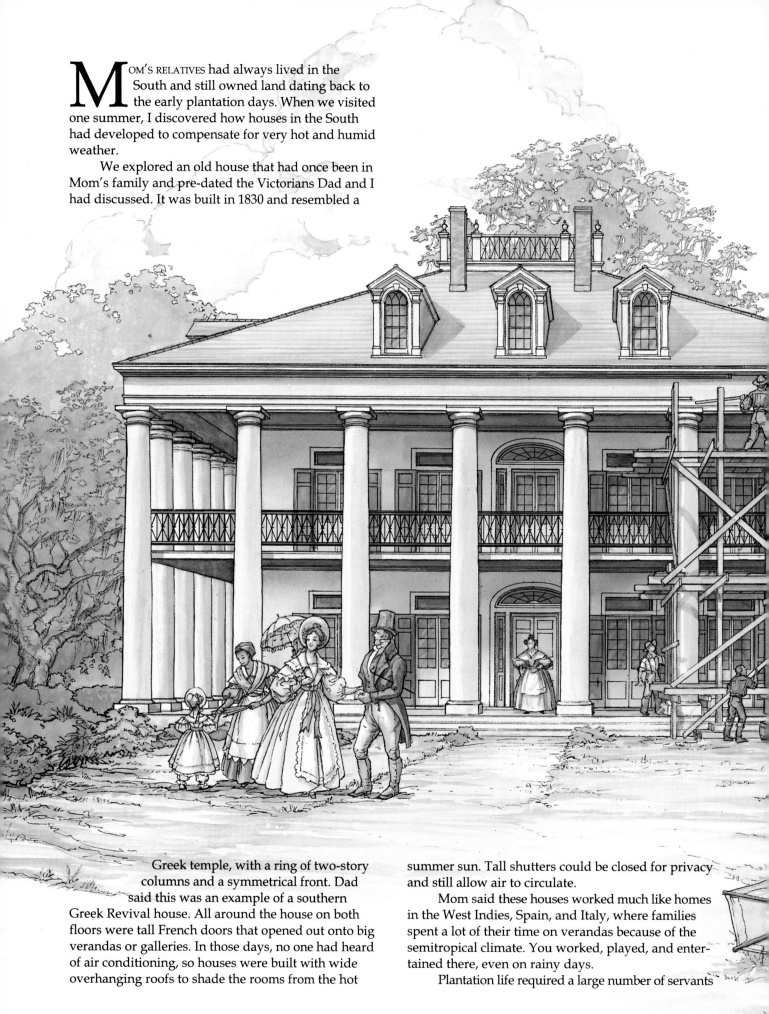

OM'S RELATIVES had always lived in the South and still owned land dating back to the early plantation days. When we visited one summer, I discovered how houses in the South had developed to compensate for very hot and humid weather.

We explored an old house that had once been in Mom's family and pre-dated the Victorians Dad and I had discussed. It was built in 1830 and resembled a

Greek temple, with a ring of two-story columns and a symmetrical front. Dad said this was an example of a southern Greek Revival house. All around the house on both floors were tall French doors that opened out onto big verandas or galleries. In those days, no one had heard of air conditioning, so houses were built with wide overhanging roofs to shade the rooms from the hot

summer sun. Tall shutters could be closed for privacy and still allow air to circulate.

Mom said these houses worked much like homes in the West Indies, Spain, and Italy, where families spent a lot of their time on verandas because of the semitropical climate. You worked, played, and entertained there, even on rainy days.

Plantation life required a large number of servants

and slaves. One thing that made meals cumbersome was the kitchen. It usually was built as a detached building, or dependency, to keep heat and smells out of the main house. This meant food didn't come to the table very hot. Servants had to run 50 to 100 feet along pathways to the house carrying covered dishes to serve the food. Often, they were made to whistle while they ran to prove they weren't tasting the food.

For Mom's ancestors, entertaining visitors was an important pastime, and most of these homes had a ballroom for parties and dances. She said they even entertained guests before the outside of the house was completely finished. It had taken three years to build because most of the workers had little time to spare from tending the plantation crops. The last summer, while trim was still being put up on the house, the first

company arrived. The plantation had prospered, and plans were already being made to remodel the floor plan to better accommodate up to 16 guests.

The daily schedule at these times would seem a little strange to us. Breakfast was served at sunrise, after which the planter or his guests went on horseback to tour the plantation. Dinner was at one o'clock, followed by a nap to avoid the afternoon's heat. Tea and cakes were served after this siesta. Later, guests dressed for supper, served at seven o'clock. Then social life really began. People visited on the verandas in soft starlight, with laughing and chatting, while in the dark yards great bonfires, started at dusk to drive away the mosquitoes and fear of sickness, burned and sparkled. Torches along the drives lighted the way for visitors and made the fronts of the grand plantation houses glow.

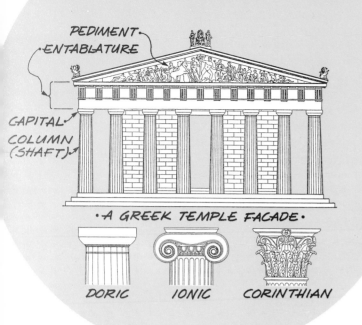

PEDIMENT
ENTABLATURE

CAPITAL
COLUMN
(SHAFT)

·A GREEK TEMPLE FACADE·

DORIC   IONIC   CORINTHIAN

the street enabling them to step down from high carriages. I especially like the horse's head post used for tying up a visitor's horse.

Because it was built before 1830, the house was very plain and simple inside, and as formal as its outside details. The walls were tinted pale colors because it would have been too expensive for most Americans in the early 1800s to buy wallpaper imported from Europe. The high-ceiling

IN THE NORTH, Greek Revival houses tended to be more formal and severe than those in the South, Dad explained. We visited a Greek Revival house whose front looked just like a Greek temple. It was very symmetrical, or balanced, in plan. It was nearly square with a wing on each side of the main house, which made it look formal and impressive. Dad said the ruins of Greek and Roman buildings were often white marble, so in the 1800s people thought the best Greek Revival houses should be painted white. The capitals of the huge columns were from the Doric order, one of the three architectural orders developed by the Greeks. The other two orders were the Ionic, which featured a scroll pattern, and the Corinthian, which included a pattern of acanthus leaves. Because it was difficult for builders to make scrolls and leaves from stone or wood, Ionic and Corinthian columns were seldom used in the United States until 1850. Then these designs could be made more easily using cast iron and stamped tin. The Greek Revival houses themselves were fairly easy for a carpenter to build, because they were based on traditional house forms with round or square columns made of wood or plastered brick.

Porches were not used as much as they were in the South, but they were still important for family activities. In winter, the family stayed inside for most work and amusements. When visitors arrived by carriage, they could use the special set of stone steps by

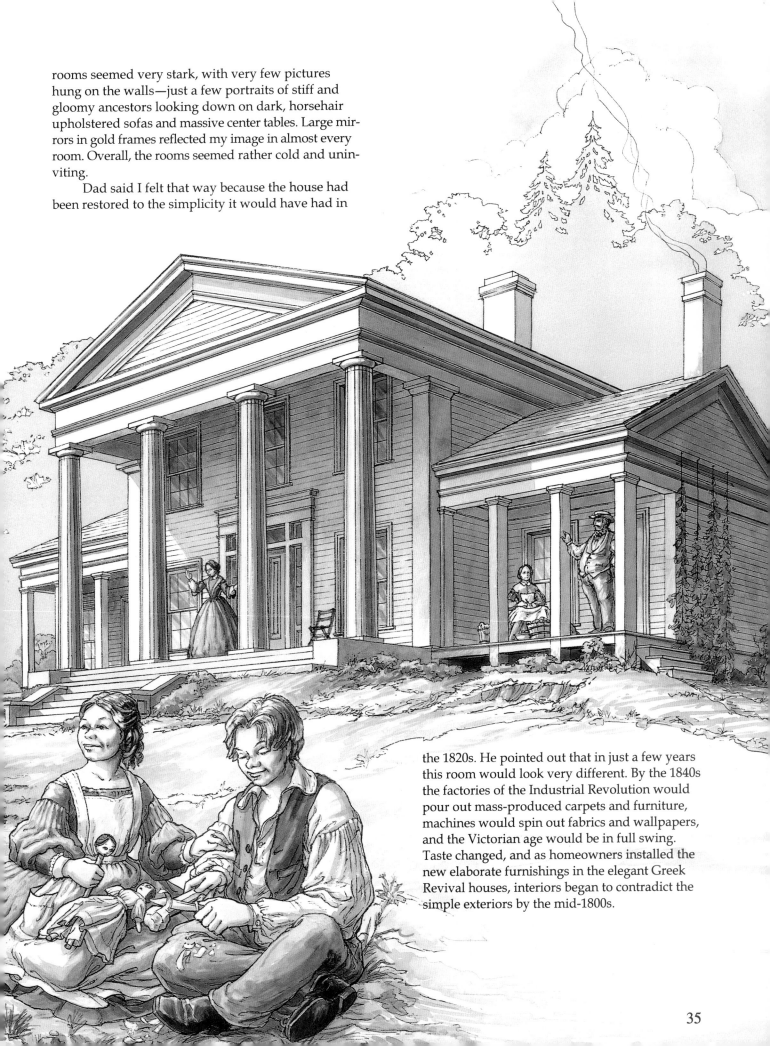

rooms seemed very stark, with very few pictures hung on the walls—just a few portraits of stiff and gloomy ancestors looking down on dark, horsehair upholstered sofas and massive center tables. Large mirrors in gold frames reflected my image in almost every room. Overall, the rooms seemed rather cold and uninviting.

Dad said I felt that way because the house had been restored to the simplicity it would have had in the 1820s. He pointed out that in just a few years this room would look very different. By the 1840s the factories of the Industrial Revolution would pour out mass-produced carpets and furniture, machines would spin out fabrics and wallpapers, and the Victorian age would be in full swing. Taste changed, and as homeowners installed the new elaborate furnishings in the elegant Greek Revival houses, interiors began to contradict the simple exteriors by the mid-1800s.

WE ALSO VISITED a restored Victorian house that was decorated in a style that Mom called "Antebellum," meaning before the Civil War. It was in the "French Taste" that Dad had talked about—very colorful, but a little fancy for me. I couldn't picture a television here.

Mom said that on a quiet Sunday afternoon, the family would have used this front parlor to entertain visitors, and children had to be on their best behavior. Neither their Sunday clothes nor the room was to be messed up. Shawls or afghans were spread to protect the carpets or upholstery from damage during play.

The parlor had a marble fireplace with a huge, gold-framed mirror over it. The wallpaper was as busy as the floral carpeting, which was sewn together from narrow strips. People back then loved to mix up patterns.

Between the tall windows with their heavy
draperies and lace curtains were a pier mirror and
console table. All of the furniture was made of dark
rosewood and upholstered in velvets and damask
(I'm learning a whole new language!). Victorians
loved to keep all of their "treasures" on display here.
The new photo album, wonderful things under glass
domes, an imported French clock, and family "fancy
work" and mementos—all were kept out for others to
admire.

Most girls took piano lessons, and the family
would gather around the square piano to sing together. Mom said parlors often smelled musty (she especially remembered her grandmother's), because
they were closed up during the week. Today
our living room is almost like a parlor, because
we spend most of our time in the family room.

GRANDDAD SHOWED ME an old, leather-bound diary that had been in the family since 1843. It was written by my great-great-grandfather's great-grandfather, Frank Houston. Granddad was very proud to have something that old handed down in the family. The handwriting was hard to read, but it described the problems my ancestors had run into when they built their first house in Michigan around 1845.

Frank Houston had bought a piece of land near a river and had had it surveyed to be sure of the property lines. He and his brother had both been carpenters and had chosen a picture and plan of a "Gothic rural residence" from Andrew Downing's book. Since they knew how to build, they simply enlarged the floor plan and laid out

•A COTTAGE IN THE RURAL GOTHIC STYLE

•A TYPICAL MEDIEVAL IDEAL
GREAT CHALFIELD MANOR – C. 1480

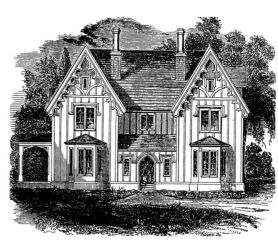

•A WOODEN CARPENTER GOTHIC COTTAG

the measurements for the foundations. We knew just what the house looked like because my ancestor had cut out the picture from Downing's book and stuck it in the diary!

Granddad said lots of houses didn't really have architects, just master carpenters who applied their knowledge to a problem as they went along. "You draw it, and I can build it," was the way they worked. They could do almost everything—framing, siding, roofing, and inside finished carpentry.

The diary explained how the Houston brothers purchased lumber from a local sawmill and ordered the foundation stone from a nearby quarry. The stone and lumber cost $175, and the mason charged $8 for 25 days' work to cut and lay the foundation. He also carved the fireplaces for the same price. Granddad

•A LARGE HOUSE IN THE POINTED STYLE

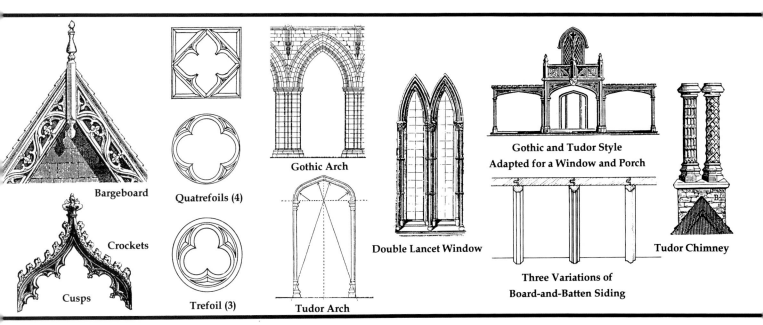

Bargeboard

Quatrefoils (4)

Gothic Arch

Double Lancet Window

Gothic and Tudor Style Adapted for a Window and Porch

Tudor Chimney

Crockets

Cusps

Trefoil (3)

Tudor Arch

Three Variations of Board-and-Batten Siding

thought that much work for so little money was a deal. We looked at a reprint of Downing's book, *Cottage Residences*, first published in 1842, which showed sketches and plans for houses ranging from modest cottages to large country villas. It told a good craftsman all he needed to know about materials, construction details, and even formulas for color and stains.

The book showed many houses designed in the Gothic Revival style, the first picturesque Victorian style to come to America in the 1840s. These houses had charm and quaint qualities in sharp contrast to the coldly formal Greek Revival style. Dad said that Gothic Revival was a hodge-podge of adaptations of details from medieval and Elizabethan buildings. The illustrations showed steep, gabled roofs trimmed with carved decorative bargeboards; pointed, lancet-shaped windows; and oriel or bay windows. Trim and brackets had

Gothic or Tudor arches edged with cusps and crockets. They were like fairy tales brought to life.

Downing liked to use stone for his houses because this was the material used by builders for important buildings in the Middle Ages. Realizing, however, that in the United States wood was more available, and easier to work, he suggested a way to use wood so it would hint of stone. His houses could be sided with vertical boards and battens and then stained a dark color or painted with a thin coat of cement to make them look like stone.

In the United States, larger, more expensive Gothic Revival homes were built with stone. Lyndhurst, designed by a friend and collaborator of Downing's, Alexander J. Davis, in Tarrytown, New York, looks like a castle with towers, battlements, and Gothic windows. I would have loved to have lived in a Davis castle.

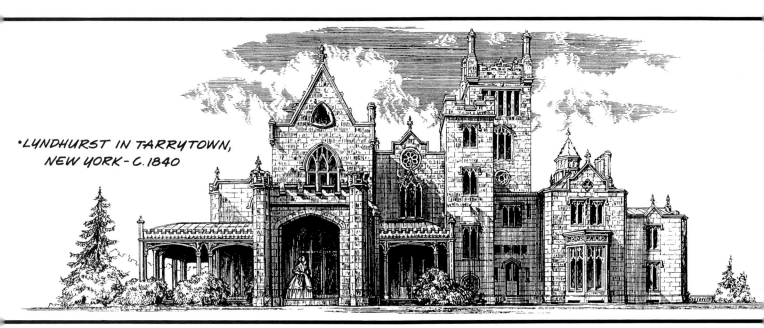

•LYNDHURST IN TARRYTOWN, NEW YORK ~ C. 1840

THE OLD DIARY also described the first Christmas in the new house in 1847. Celebrations lasted 12 days, and it was a wonderfully busy time with several house guests. More relatives came for Christmas dinner, arriving on horseback or by sleigh because of a heavy snow. The house must have smelled delicious to the arriving guests because 12 mince pies had been baked that day. The day after Christmas, on Boxing Day, a special party was given

Gothic Revival Privy

for friends and servants, while another on Epiphany Eve included a Twelfth Night cake filled with raisins, nuts, candied fruit, and hidden coins.

German immigrant neighbors brought my relatives a special housewarming present—their first Christmas tree. Not many families had trees, and the decorations consisted of spice and gingerbread cookies, bits of ribbon, and tinsel.

Throughout the holiday, fires burned in all the fireplaces, the only means of heat except in the kitchen where the new, cast-iron stove (the first in the county, bragged the diary) was kept lighted for cooking all day long.

Mom thought feeding guests three meals a day must have kept the women and older girls very busy. She said there would have been many trips to the dependencies, or out-buildings, that stored various provisions. Few homes had full basements until the late 19th century, so a root cellar, dug in the back yard, was used to store apples, potatoes, carrots, cabbages, and other winter vegetables. A smokehouse would have held the cured hams and bacon from fall butchering. A spring, or milk house, kept the family's

milk and cream. The house described in the diary also had a larder, a small, unheated room that Dad said was just off the kitchen to store food in a cool place in summer and to keep food from freezing in winter. The diary listed what was stored in the larder that fall: crocks of pickles, barrels of salted and pickled meat, jugs of molasses and maple syrup, extra bread and pies. Barrels of flour and cornmeal were stored against being snowed in. The ceiling was hung with strings of dried fruit, herbs, and cured hams. The larder would have been a room full of wonderful smells.

A carriage house and barn together provided shelter for horses and protected sleighs and carriages. Older boys of the household would have been responsible for the feeding and care for all the guests' horses. Paths also had to be shoveled, wood brought in, and ashes carried out.

This new house included a Gothic-style outdoor privy, which must have provided a very chilly experience in the winter. At night, chamber pots were kept in each bedroom for emergencies and had to be emptied and scrubbed in the morning. The most constant task was bringing in water from the outside well and emptying the bath and

dish water. This all meant plenty of daily chores to keep the entire family busy when company stayed.

The new house, with its cozy Gothic interior, had been brought to life with family and friends. Frank Houston wrote in his diary, "Our hard work was rewarded by a most joyous first Christmas in our new home with everyone entering heartily into the festivities. I nearly tuckered myself out between shoveling snow and talking farming and politics."

Wondrous New Cast-Iron Stove

GRANDMA SAID she could take us even farther back in time and showed us a framed, cross-stitched sampler handed down in her family. An alphabet and a house decorated the sampler along with the words "Sara Ladermann wrought this sampler—age 10—Georgetown 1810." Beneath the house were these words: "Our Merchant's Home." Grandma explained that little girls did this kind of project for practice when they were learning needlework.

Grandma showed us photographs she had taken in Washington, D.C., of the house that had been Sara's

home. She called it a Federal town house, a style built for nearly 50 years after the American Revolution in 1776. These houses were also laid out like English terrace houses just as Aunt Margaret's brownstone had been: three floors high with service rooms in the basement and gardens at the rear. Downstairs off the entrance hall was a double drawing room (they weren't called parlors yet) and a dining room over the basement kitchen. The upstairs bedrooms and nursery were the private parts of the house.

Grandma said this type of house was a simpler version of an English style created by the Adam

ABCDEFGHI
KLMNOPQR
STUVWXYZ

Sara Ladermann Wrought
this sampler + age 10

George   town 1810
IIIIVX

+ Our Merchant's Home +

brothers. They had studied Roman architecture in Italy and used the classical elements they saw there in a new way by executing delicate patterns of columns, urns, swags, and garlands in carvings and plasterwork. Grandma said in the United States the Adam influence could chiefly be seen in interior decoration and looked very formal and restrained—just the sort of taste her prosperous merchant relatives would have liked.

There were three girls in the family: Sara, Ellen, and Lauren. Grandma had us imagine one of their favorite kinds of afternoons. The three girls would have tea with their mother in her bedroom, while their father entertained other merchants on business downstairs in the front drawing room. A tea table was set with the best china, and their mother would pour tea-milk, served with little cakes or jam tarts. Sometimes their favorite treats—snickerdoodles, small sugar cookies with chopped nuts—would be served. During this special time of day manners were learned and secrets shared. The youngest child, Lauren, was allowed to bring a favorite doll to play with, but most toys were kept in the nursery, which also was the girls' classroom.

Children seldom were allowed to play in the front of town houses such as this, because there were no front gardens and the unpaved streets could be muddy and the horses dangerous. Instead, back gardens became private playgrounds and quiet green retreats for the family.

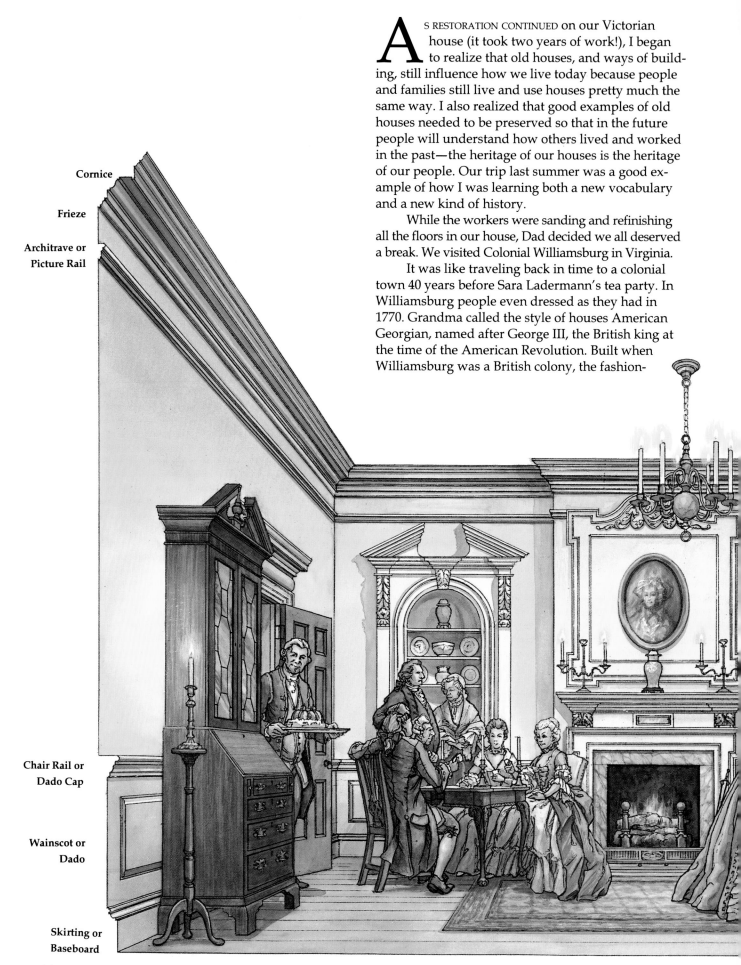

Cornice

Frieze

Architrave or
Picture Rail

Chair Rail or
Dado Cap

Wainscot or
Dado

Skirting or
Baseboard

AS RESTORATION CONTINUED on our Victorian house (it took two years of work!), I began to realize that old houses, and ways of building, still influence how we live today because people and families still live and use houses pretty much the same way. I also realized that good examples of old houses needed to be preserved so that in the future people will understand how others lived and worked in the past—the heritage of our houses is the heritage of our people. Our trip last summer was a good example of how I was learning both a new vocabulary and a new kind of history.

While the workers were sanding and refinishing all the floors in our house, Dad decided we all deserved a break. We visited Colonial Williamsburg in Virginia.

It was like traveling back in time to a colonial town 40 years before Sara Ladermann's tea party. In Williamsburg people even dressed as they had in 1770. Grandma called the style of houses American Georgian, named after George III, the British king at the time of the American Revolution. Built when Williamsburg was a British colony, the fashionable homes followed English styles inside and out. The Georgian style is still popular today, Grandma noted, because it uses well-designed traditional house forms in a pleasing way.

In a prosperous merchant's house, Grandma had us imagine a New Year's Eve party. Two grand drawing rooms would have been opened for the occasion, with the two fireplaces ablaze and all the candles lighted. Some tables would have been set up for playing cards. Guests, even the grownups, might have played blindman's buff, followed by jovial toasts of egg nog or hot wine punch and small cakes and cookies. The guests probably toasted the king. While friends talked, the children would share their Christmas toys, then beg their parents to stay up late, just like today.

Grandma said burning so many candles for a long party would have been very expensive and was not done except on special occasions. People may have dressed differently then, but families and friends celebrated in pretty much the same way.

GRANDMA WAS INTERESTED in our family's genealogy, the tracing of our family tree. The earliest relatives that she could track down were a branch of the family who had lived near Philadelphia, the largest and most fashionable city in the colonies, before the American Revolution.

Grandma found records of the family of Francis Houston, a merchant lawyer who must have liked to write letters because he left so many. She showed us copies she had made at the local historical

house suitable to a "fashionable Englishman of means." He had seen Palladian houses in England that he felt were ideal. Palladian architecture, Grandma explained, was another style that used classical elements—only they were heavier and bolder. It was funny, she said, but every few generations, someone proposed a new version of classical architecture that claimed to be the most accurate and the best.

Grandma showed us pictures of the house. It had an imposing facade faced with ashlar made of native stone. The facade was broken by a projecting center section with an entrance graced by Doric columns

society. They were like Granddad's diary and let you peek through a window in time. I read about Houston's studies in London and his prosperous business, both there and in America. He even became involved in politics and, as his business and reputation grew, built an impressive country house outside the city.

He wrote a friend that he was going to build a

topped by a classical pediment. Another pediment projected from the roofline. Two dependencies were set slightly to the rear. I thought the house looked imposing with its bold details, such as the urn shapes decorating the roof, which were very different from Sara's modest Federal town house. Houston had built a house that was a tribute to his position.

After a snowstorm in winter it could take more than two hours to travel the six miles by horse and cutter to the city. Cut off for days, the household would have to rely on its own store of supplies. The only heat would have been from the eight fireplaces, and, Houston wrote, "the upstairs bedrooms were left unheated for economy, and healthy sleep." The wide, pineboard floors would have really been cold on bare feet, if you didn't happen to step on a throw rug in the morning.

The letters told us stories of important visitors to the house, who often stayed overnight because they were "so far from the city." Such a large house required servants, according to Grandma. They prepared meals over an open hearth, tended the fireplaces, did laundry by hand, and swept and dusted daily. They also trimmed or replaced as many as 50 candles a day. A housewife needed a lot of help.

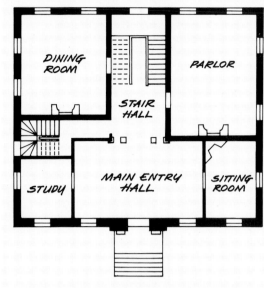

· PLAN of MAIN HOUSE FIRST FLOOR ·

I THOUGHT IT WAS TERRIBLE to tear down the additions on our Victorian house, but Dad said they really didn't fit with the style of the original house. Sometimes additions do work, Dad pointed out. In fact, many old houses weren't always built complete at one time—they often grew. He said this didn't have to result in a patchwork house. When well planned, the final home could be totally unified.

Dad drew a diagram of a typical early colonial house in Massachusetts to show how it might have evolved over the years. The first part of the house might have been built about 1670. It probably had only one ground floor room with a huge fireplace and a cramped stair to one room above, topped by an attic loft. Twenty years later, as the family grew, the easiest enlargement was to add to the length by building on two new rooms on the other side of the chimney and stair.

About 1700 a saltbox addition at the rear created two more rooms. As the family prospered, a major rebuilding could have unified the house 50 years later. By then the house would have grown to 10 rooms with the addition of one more room's length, a large attic-loft, and the completion of the lean-to at the rear.

Dad said the final modification could have come about 1780, with an extension topped by a gabled roof, new entry porch, siding, and shutters. He was right; it looked very unified and well planned.

On the inside, ceilings were very low—often barely seven feet high—to preserve heat. The main

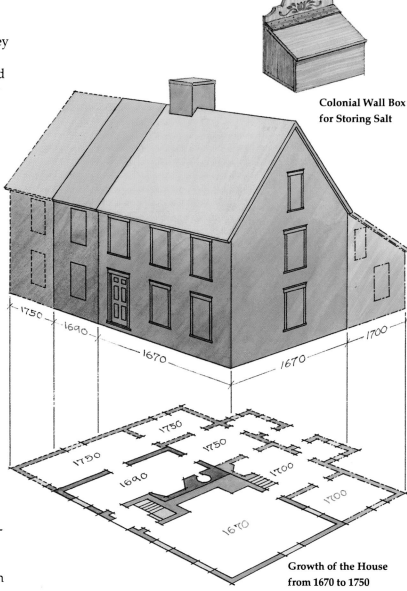

Colonial Wall Box for Storing Salt

Growth of the House from 1670 to 1750

Complete House c. 1780

big room, called a hall or keeping room, would have served as a combined room for cooking, dining, living, and, often, sleeping. A huge spacious fireplace—sometimes more than eight feet wide—dominated the room. An oven was built into the rear or side brickwork forming the fireplace. In the fireplace, a lug-pole or iron crane would have supported the chains and hooks used to suspend kettles and pots for cooking. Spits and gridirons were used for roasting meats, and special long-handled pans and griddles were used for frying over an open fire. Most meals consisted of boiled meat, corn mush, vegetables, and stews, along with breads baked in the oven or in front of the fire. Cooking was slow, arduous work, requiring a practiced eye and hand.

Nearly every house had a garden, and lucky families kept a cow for milk and cream, which could be churned into butter.

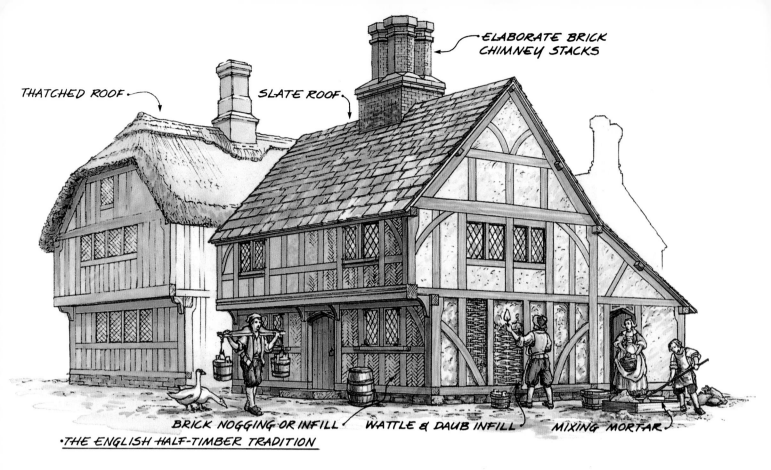

THATCHED ROOF

SLATE ROOF

ELABORATE BRICK CHIMNEY STACKS

BRICK NOGGING OR INFILL   WATTLE & DAUB INFILL   MIXING MORTAR

•THE ENGLISH HALF-TIMBER TRADITION

COLONIAL HOUSES were a lot less sophisticated than our huge Victorian Second Empire home. We have more comforts and space for different activities, including lots of closets. Dad explained that the first English colonists were struggling to survive, and they continued to build in the only way they knew, in the European, late-medieval tradition. Building a house of wood and brick in the 1600s was slow and difficult: timber had to be found, cut, and trimmed, and clay for bricks dug, formed, then fired in kiln ovens.

Dad said they built the same kind of timber-framed houses in England that we had a picture of on our sample board—framing a house with timber, then filling in the spaces between the timbers and studs with brick, stone, or wattle and daub (clay over a basketwork of boughs). Dad called this "half-timbering." In England, these filled-in areas often were left exposed or covered with plaster or stucco, but in the colonies they were covered with shingles or clapboards because of more severe weather. For the same reason, wood shingles proved more durable for roofs than English thatching.

In the New England colonies, these houses with steep roofs usually had only one room on either side of a huge central fireplace. A curious feature was that

•ENGLISH -ABOUT 1610

•DETAIL OF COMPLEX JOINTS OF 2ND FLOOR JETTY AT MAIN CORNER POSTS

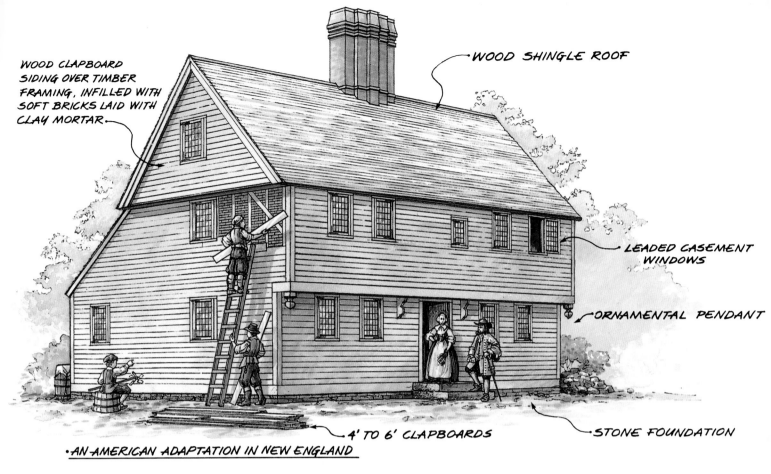

WOOD CLAPBOARD SIDING OVER TIMBER FRAMING, INFILLED WITH SOFT BRICKS LAID WITH CLAY MORTAR

WOOD SHINGLE ROOF

LEADED CASEMENT WINDOWS

ORNAMENTAL PENDANT

4' TO 6' CLAPBOARDS

STONE FOUNDATION

• AN AMERICAN ADAPTATION IN NEW ENGLAND

the second-story rooms often overhung the lower story on the front. Dad said this was done by making upper-floor timbers project out over the lower walls. These overhangs sometimes had decorative carved pendants at the corners. The lean-to additions in the back, to provide more space, gave the houses the look of traditional saltboxes.

The inside of these early homes was very cozy. A huge fireplace was the focus of each room. The fire was kept going throughout the day for warmth, cooking, and light. Except for the light from the fire, the interiors, with only a few small windows, were dark; glass was hard to make and was expensive.

Dad said the furniture was very limited and strictly practical—tables, chests, stools, benches, and very few chairs. I don't think I'd have liked the early, packed-earth floors that Dad talked about; later floors of stone or wood planks would have been better, even if they were left bare.

Ever since the colonists, Dad noted, 16 generations of Americans have built houses largely following the traditions of their European homelands. Even our Second Empire Victorian was based on some of these early traditions.

BLANKET CRANE

A CHILD'S PADDED "PUDDING-HEAD" CAP, WORN TO HELP PROTECT FROM BUMPS

STRAPS FOR ADJUSTING WINDOWS

• AMERICAN - ABOUT 1690

51

OUR "NEW" HOUSE smelled of fresh paint and varnish on moving day, and there was new wallpaper every where. It had taken nearly two years to restore our house to the point that Mom agreed we could move in. There were still some things to do like getting some of the upstairs rooms painted, but Mom wanted to get settled in before winter. Without furniture, the house was kind of echoey inside.

Everyone in the family had moving-day "jitters." Mom and Dad especially worried about everything. Would the movers scratch the finish on the parquet floor in the front hall or scrape the new wallpaper on the staircase wall? Mom fussed over where the furniture was to be placed. Dad grumbled about carrying heavy furniture upstairs.

Just as I was feeling homesick for our old house, the last of our familiar furniture was moved in. I had felt suspended between two worlds and was glad to see my bed and desk in my new, huge bedroom. I really

had wanted Lisa's tower bedroom, but she won the coin toss, and I settled for this room for its size.

Mom said we could send out for pizza the first night—she was too tired to hunt through boxes in the kitchen and cook. Dad thought we could "lay a fire" in the dining room fireplace to make things festive for our first dinner. We decided that, afterward, we would have enough strength to hang some pictures to make us all feel at home. Lisa had disappeared and then suddenly announced loudly from the top of the stairs that she had counted the steps from the basement to the attic. There were 104 steps on the front stair and 82 on the steep back stairs! Lisa always likes number things!

Just then, the doorbell rang, and there were Granddad and Grandma and 10 of our neighbors. They had all watched us restore the house and wanted to see the results. Some even brought pictures they had taken of the restoration in progress to share with us. It was great to have these new friends, especially because they brought along food to welcome us to our "new" home. We all had a feast in the dining room and didn't miss the pizza. Then Mom led a "grand tour" of every room. We never did get the pictures hung.

Was I ever tired at the end of moving day! The floor in my bedroom had a nice little squeak and my favorite rug wasn't on the floor yet, but we could do that the next day. That first night Lisa got scared because she didn't have curtains in her tower bedroom, and tree branches made strange shadows on her walls. I told her we could trade rooms, but no deal.

Fixing up this new old house has been an adventure, just like Dad promised, and I bet it will still have some surprises. I feel like I've built it myself . . . with a little help from everyone else, of course. Now our house is ready to face another hundred or two years. And I've got a huge room, my cozy bed, clean sheets, a plump pillow. I guess I'd better say "Goodnight!"

Glossary

Arcade A series of arches supported by columns or posts.

Ashlar Squared, cut stone laid regularly in parallel courses.

Bay window A window of one or two stories projecting from the face of a building at ground level.

Belt course Narrow horizontal band projecting from the exterior walls of buildings, usually defining interior floor levels.

Bracket A projecting support element under eaves or shelves, often more decorative than functional.

Clapboards Long, narrow horizontal boards, overlapped to cover outer walls of framed buildings. Also called weatherboard.

Cretonne A heavy, unglazed cotton or linen fabric printed in colored patterns for drapery or upholstery use.

Crystal radio set An early form of radio receiver having a crystal detector but no electron tubes.

Cupola A small roofed structure projecting from the top of a roof, built on a square or round base.

Cutter A one-horse sleigh.

Damask Drapery or upholstery fabric made on a mechanical loom with lustrous reversible patterns or figures.

Davenport suite A set of matched upholstered furniture, sold as a whole and consisting of a sofa and matching armchair.

Dependency Any building separate from the house it is designed to serve, such as a detached kitchen or servant's quarters.

Dormer A small gabled window projecting from a sloping roof.

Eaves The projecting overhang at the lower edge of a roof.

Facade The face or main front of a building.

Floor plan A flat architectural plan showing the arrangement of rooms and other spaces on one floor of a building.

Foundation That part of a building or wall, partly or wholly below ground, that serves as its base.

Gable The upper, triangular portion of a wall at the end of a ridged roof.

Gingerbread Elaborate wooden fretwork or scrollwork patterns used on gables or as porch trim and common on 19th-century domestic buildings.

Gramophone A trademark name for early talking machines and records. An early form of record player.

Header A structural member fastened between vertical framing members to support ends of joists, rafters, or studding.

Hip roof A roof that slopes upward from all four sides of a building.

Ice box An early nonmechanical form of a refrigerator, using blocks of ice for cooling.

Jig saw A slim saw with a vertical blade for cutting curved or irregular lines with a reciprocating action.

Laths Narrow wood strips used to support plaster over wood framing.

Lathe A machine used to shape wood by cutting with a fixed blade on a horizontal axis.

Linoleum A 19th- and early 20th-century floor covering material, made of oxidized linseed oil and cork pressed on canvas or burlap.

Oilcloth A fabric waterproofed with oils and pigments and used as a table covering.

Oriel window A window projecting from the flat face of a wall on an upper story.

Out building A building separate from and subordinate to a main building, as a woodshed or barn to a house.

Parquet Wood flooring with an inlaid mosaic pattern.

Phonograph An early record player.

Picturesque During the mid-18th to early 19th centuries, a term describing a scene, object, or structure that had a striking, irregular beauty, charm, or quaintness.

Plaster A pasty mixture of sand, lime, and water used for coating walls and ceilings.

Quoin Unit of cut stone or brick used to accentuate the vertical corners of buildings.

Sash A frame in which the glass panes of a window are set.

Scrollwork Ornamental work with curvilinear open patterns.

Slate A hard, fine-grained gray stone, easily split into thin layers, used to make roofing shingles.

Spindle A turned, vertical wooden element used in stair railings, porch trim, and furniture.

Stucco A mixture of portland cement, lime, and sand mixed with water; used to cover a building's exterior walls; also, plaster of fine quality for interior molding and modeling.

Thatching A roof covering made of reeds or straw.

Tracery Interlaced lines that form the lacy openwork of a Gothic-style window.

Tract development A planned land area or community of homes usually promoted by a developer or contracting firm.

Varnish A protective coating for wood made of resins and oils or volatile solvents.

Wilton carpet A type of carpet with a cut-loop velvet-like face.

Wing A part of a building projecting from and subordinate to the main or central part.

Zinc lining A soft, nonrusting metal lining used to waterproof the interiors of sinks and bathtubs in the 19th century.

MICHAEL GAUGHENBAUGH is a free-lance writer and historian with major interests and background in American political history and the European royal families.

HERBERT L. CAMBURN has been a professional stage and costume designer and educator for 38 years and is currently head of the theater design program at California State University at Long Beach.

Both author and illustrator grew up in the Midwest with its rich heritage of 19th-century architecture and are ardent architectural historians and conservationists.